KINGDOM

Slimy Sea Monsters

SEA OF SECRETS

LAKE OF MYSTERY

Scary
cave beasts

PEAKS OF PERIL

For my two littlest sisters,
Lilac and Freya, the smartest,
bravest, and strongest girls I know.

—B. W.

Published by
PEACHTREE PUBLISHING COMPANY INC.
1700 Chattahoochee Avenue
Atlanta, Georgia 30318-2112
www.peachtree-online.com

Text and illustrations © 2020 by Bethan Woollvin
First published in Great Britain in 2020 by Two Hoots, an imprint of Pan Macmillan
First United States version published in 2020 by Peachtree Publishing Company Inc.

The illustrations were rendered in gouache on cartridge paper.

Printed in September 2019 in China
10 9 8 7 6 5 4 3 2 1
First Edition

HC ISBN: 978-1-68263-182-9

Cataloging-in-Publication Data is available from the Library of Congress.

BO THE BRAVE

Bethan Woollvin

PEACHTREE

ATLANTA

Bo lived with her older brothers,
Erik and Ivar, in a land of
mountains and forests.

Erik and Ivar were hunters, and one day they set off on a quest to catch a monster.

"Please, can I come with you? I want to catch a monster too!" begged Bo.

"You must stay at home!" said Ivar.

"Besides," Erik sneered.
"You're far too little."

MONSTER

SPOTTED

Bo went to her room and sulked.

I'm not too little, she thought.

I'm smart and brave and strong!

And so Bo crept out of the castle to catch a monster of her own.

Deep in the forest, Bo caught a glimpse of a strange creature.

"Beware, you horrid monster! I'm Bo the Brave!" she shouted, as she quickly drew an arrow and aimed. "Get ready to be got!"

"Me? A monster? Certainly not!" the creature replied. "I'm the Griffin. Now lower your bow. I mean you no harm!"

Bo was suspicious. The Griffin *looked* like a monster.

"You seem lost. Can I help you find your way?" he asked
politely.

He is far too helpful to be a monster, thought Bo.
So she told the Griffin about her quest.

"I heard the sea is full of monsters!" the Griffin said.

And so they set off to find one.

It wasn't long before they spotted
another strange creature.

"Beware, you slimy monster!
I'm Bo the Brave."

Bo stretched out to capture the beast beneath the waves.

"Get ready to be—" But she leaned over too far and toppled overboard.

"You simply simply MUST learn to swim," the sea creature bellowed, plucking Bo from the waves. "And me? A monster? Don't be ridiculous. I am the Kraken! I mean you no harm."

Bo was suspicious. The Kraken *looked* like a
monster and *smelled* like a monster, but a true
monster wouldn't have saved her.

She is far too nice to be a monster, thought Bo.
So Bo told the Kraken about her quest.

"I heard that monsters live in caves!"
the Kraken said. And so they set off
to find one.

Well, now! This creature *looked* like a monster, and it *smelled* like a monster—and, goodness! It certainly *sounded* like a scary monster!

ROAR

But as Bo crept closer, she noticed something odd.
Instead of being angry, the creature
was crying!

"I'm sorry," said Bo. "I didn't mean to upset you.
I thought you were a monster."

"No, I'm just a dragon," a deep voice replied. "And *you* haven't upset me. My poor baby was stolen, and I can't find him anywhere!"

She is far too caring to be a monster, thought Bo.

"I can help, I'm Bo the Brave! And I think I know *just* where we can find your baby…"

Bo and her new friends swooped off to look
for the Dragon's baby.

"My baby must be over there," cried the Dragon. "He always gets fiery when he's scared!"

And so they headed up toward the burning castle.

As they landed, Bo spotted her brothers, Erik and Ivar.

They didn't look or smell or sound like monsters…

but they were certainly *acting* like monsters!

"Beware, you nasty beasts!" shouted Bo. "I'm Bo the Brave! Get ready to be got!" And with that, she threw water over the flames—and her monstrous brothers.

"Let that baby dragon go!" yelled Bo. "These creatures are helpful and nice and caring. We shouldn't be hunting them!"

Erik and Ivar were so relieved
not to have been eaten that they
agreed never to go monster
hunting again.

From then on, Bo loved roaming the land and learning about all the amazing creatures she came across—with the help of her brothers, of course.

Because Bo wasn't too little.
She was smart, she was strong...

she was Bo the Brave.

ALPINE

home

monster
My ~~stinky~~
brothers

ALPINE CASTLE

The griffin
Horrid
~~forest
monsters~~

FRIGHTFUL FOREST